For Annie, Daniel, Charley, Nick and Ruth,
and all the other babies who know best K.H.

For Björn with love   B.G.

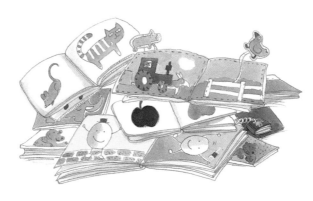

TRANSWORLD PUBLISHERS
61-63 Uxbridge Road, London W5 5SA
A division of The Random House Group Ltd

RANDOM HOUSE AUSTRALIA (PTY) LTD
20 Alfred St, Milsons Point, Sydney,
New South Wales 2061, Australia

RANDOM HOUSE NEW ZEALAND LTD
18 Poland Rd, Glenfield, Auckland 10, New Zealand

RANDOM HOUSE (PTY) LTD
Endulini, 5a Jubilee Road, Parktown 2193, South Africa

Published in 2001 by Doubleday
a division of Transworld Publishers

Text Copyright © Kathy Henderson 2001
Illustrations Copyright © Brita Granström 2001

Designed by Ian Butterworth

The right of Kathy Henderson to be identified
as the Author and the right of Brita Granström to be
identified as the Illustrator of this work has
been asserted in accordance with the
Copyright, Designs and Patents Act 1988

A catalogue record for this book is available
from the British Library

ISBN 0 385 600704

Printed in Singapore

Baby Knows Best

Kathy Henderson
Illustrated by Brita Granström

DOUBLEDAY

We gave the baby rattles
and we gave her things with bells,
she's got toys that roll and click and tick,
there's one that sings as well,
she's got a posting box that whistles
and a squeaky mouse to squeeze...

And what does she want to play with?

The front door keys.

She's got a rag book about farms
that's full of ducks and pigs and goats,
she's got my old book of nursery rhymes,
and a plastic book that floats,
she's got books with cardboard pages
and bright pictures just for her...

And what does she want to look at?

The newspaper.

Grandpa brought a bath toy
that's got sieves and scoops inside,
he brought a wind-up swimming hippo
with a mouth that opens wide,
she already had a tug boat
and a duck-shaped glug-glug jug...

But what does she want at bath time?

The old bath plug.

She's got dungarees and trousers,
she's got nappies, tights and socks,
she's got a bright pink quilted snowsuit
and two flower-patterned smocks,
she's got more clothes than we have
even though she's very small. . .

And what does she like wearing best?

Nothing at all.

W e mash up ripe bananas
and turn carrots into soup,
we buy jars of special baby mush
and powdered packet gloop,
we give her teething rusks and finger food
and she just drops the lot. . .

Cos what d'you think she wants to eat?

What we've got.

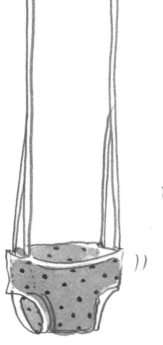

She's got a buggy and a back-pack
and a carrycot on wheels,
then there's her car seat with the handle
and the string of coloured bells
and her high chair and her bouncer
and her cot. There's all this stuff...

And where does she want to be?

Snuggled up with us.